Volume I

Pulling Back the Curtain

Ed Okonowicz

Myst and Lace Publishers
Elkton, Maryland

Spirits Between the Bays
Volume I
Pulling Back the Curtain
First Edition

ISBN 0-9643244-0-7

Published by
Myst and Lace Publishers
1386 Fair Hill Lane
Elkton, Maryland 21921

Printed in the U.S.A.
by Cedar Tree Press

Typography, Design and Illustrations
by Kathleen Okonowicz

Dedications

To my parents,
Theresa and Ed, who taught me that good things
are the result of hard work and persistence.
Ed Okonowicz

To my parents,
especially my Mom,
who always wanted me to pursue art.
Kathleen Burgoon Okonowicz

Acknowledgements

The author and illustrator appreciate the assistance of those
who have been an important part of this project.
Special thanks are extended to:

*Graphic designer and artist Boni Nash for her
advice and consultations.
*Delaware writer Sue Moncure for her
editing and valuable suggestions.
*Monica Witkowski for her reading and comments.
*The newspaper editors who published the author's
initial announcement seeking stories from Delmarva residents.
*The bookstore owners and managers
who offered important advice, especially Maxim Dadoun,
Diane Zabenko, and Lanny Parks.
*Those citizens of Delmarva who willingly shared
their ghostly experiences.

Also available from
Myst and Lace Publishers

Spirits Between the Bays Series

Volume I
Pulling Back the Curtain
(October, 1994)

Volume II
Opening the Door
(March, 1995)

Volume III
Welcome Inn
(September, 1995)

Volume IV
In the Vestibule
(Fall, 1996)

* * * *

Stairway over the Brandywine
A *Love Story*
(February, 1995)

* * * *

Possessed Possessions:
Haunted Antiques, Furniture and Collectibles
(Spring, 1996)

Table of Contents

True Stories

Legends and Lore

Introduction

I was born on Halloween Eve. To me, that end of October holiday—with frost in the air, falling leaves and dark shadows lurking in every alleyway—was more fascinating and exciting than Christmas. Perhaps that's why, as a freelance newspaper and magazine writer, I sought out stories about haunted places, lively ghosts and searchers of spirits.

Eventually, I became a professional storyteller and was intrigued by books of ghost stories written by authors located throughout the country. I realized that, while what I was reading was fascinating, similar events had occurred in the area where I lived. I also knew that some of the tales of which I had written were as mysterious as those in distant states.

I began using my own material in my storytelling programs, and I decided to seek out others, in Delaware and Maryland, who had unusual experiences and were willing to share them.

The results were satisfying. People called me and sent letters. Some talked about friendly, family ghosts they wanted to keep. Others shared horrifying experiences they wished they could forget.

* * * *

Pulling Back the Curtain is the result of these personal stories and my own earlier interviews.

As the title signifies, this book is the first volume of a series entitled *Spirits Between the Bays*, which is about the people—and spectral visitors—in the water towns, farms, crossroads, hamlets and cities on the Delmarva Peninsula.

This series will focus on:

*Unusual events that have occurred, and continue to happen,
*Strange beings that reside on the peninsula and
*Experiences of people who reside between the bays.

Most of these incidents have happened, but there also are local legends that have been told from generation to generation, until they have arrived to us in their present form.

The Peninsula

The Delmarva Peninsula—which encompasses the entire state of Delaware, nine counties of Maryland called The Eastern Shore, and two counties of Virginia—is a treasure trove of lore and legend. For centuries, American Indians walked the beaches of the Atlantic and the shores of the Chesapeake. They left their indelible mark, ancient culture and mysterious beliefs on the virgin wetlands. Later, European pioneers arrived, bringing the folkways and customs of their Old World, to establish settlements on the shorelines of both the Delaware and Chesapeake Bays.

Delmarva's coasts, inlets, highways, backroads and hidden lanes have been traveled by pirates and politicians, farmers and statesmen, robbers and rebels, watermen and witches, slaves and soldiers. Almost a secluded entity to itself—and with little regard for the changing boundaries of the area's states, cites and towns—this fascinating peninsula's citizens have traveled among the three states and played major roles in both the American Revolution and the War Between the States.

For generations, the lives on Delmarva have reflected the beauty of life, the tensions of love, the horrors of war and the mysteries of death. There have been murders and battles, duels and deceit, natural disasters and human tragedies—all balanced by memorable moments of success and happiness.

These millions of human experiences have blended to create a distinctive culture between the bays. In subtle and, at times, in noticeable ways, unexplainable fragments of the past and its spirit world have been able to push themselves into the present and make unforgettable impressions.

Oftentimes, when these unusual events or unearthly beings are noticed, many "logical" witnesses jokingly question their own sanity, or simply deny that such incidents have occurred. But the strange does happen, and these events are especially difficult to deny when they arrive on our own doorstep.

The People

Among us are people who have had full-length, feature visits from the unearthly or have seen the illogical, the bizarre and the horrifying. Some live in fear from the effects of being selected as involuntary players in the mysteries of the afterlife. Others find it fascinating and want more.

Their stories are in this book.

They are presented as they were told to me. In most cases, names have been changed to preserve the privacy of those who demonstrated their trust.

I met with these people whose stories I tell in their homes, in restaurants, at offices and on park benches.

They did not live in dark castles or century old mansions. Most went home each night to a standard suburban rancher or a simple city row house. They spend their days as artists, entrepreneurs, truck drivers, retired military personnel, engineers, homemakers, counselors, nurses, musicians, custodians and educators.

Some were nervous; others were concerned—both for themselves and for their families. A few experiences were amusing. Many were frightening. Some spirit contacts have continued for years. For others, it had been years since their last unusual encounter.

Not one person was able to provide an answer as to why he of she was selected to see or hear what others are not able, or allowed, to notice. But each person wanted his or her particular story told. And each had a personal reason as to why.

Upon the conclusion of my interview with Martin, an artist in Rehoboth Beach, Delaware, I asked him if it had been a difficult decision to call me and share his story.

Without hesitation, he said, "No." He had been involved in a strange incident nearly 10 years before, and he wanted others to be aware of it.

I asked him, "Why?"

He said, quite calmly, as if he knew the question was coming, "For years now, I've been learning that the most important things are those that are unseen. I thought sharing what had happened to me might help others who may have experienced something unusual. It also might enable them to share it with others, or find peace with themselves."

* * * *

I hope you find these stories interesting, chilling and unnerving.

My wish is that they cause your hair to stand on end, that a chill will climb up your spine, that you find it necessary to check the lock on your door and the latch on your window, that you will spend time searching for the cause of that unexplainable squeak on the stairs, that you will think about what might be . . . not only what you can see.

Most of all, I hope if you have a story to tell, you will contact me and share your encounter with the unusual. For I, and the readers of upcoming volumes of *Spirits Between the Bays*, are extremely interested in hearing about your personal contact with the unexplained.

—Ed Okonowicz,
in Fair Hill, Maryland, at the
northern edge of the Delmarva Peninsula
—October 1994

Room Full of Roses

Loretta Murphy was resting in her bed. It was dark, but not late. Her husband Henry was out for the evening, playing cards with the guys.

She was propped up against a few pillows, making it easier for her to read. Two-year-old Eric was asleep beside her. He liked to spend time in his mother's room.

The movement entered the outside corner of her left eye. It was solid, medium gray. That was the color of the old farm-style dress. Her hair, that of the strange lady's, was mainly black, but with a heavy dose of gray.

She moved without giving the slightest sound. As if her feet didn't touch the carpeting. But it wasn't a floating motion. She was taking actual steps, but there was no rustling sound of clothing.

Loretta held her breath. Keeping her head totally still and, using only her eyes, she watched the older woman's figure move evenly and swiftly across the bedroom, go into the hall and turn toward the living room.

Scared but curious, Loretta jumped out of bed and ran to the doorway, turned her head to the left, and looked down the short hallway.

Nothing.

No sound. No figure. No movement.

Quickly, she searched the living room, kitchen and other rooms of the seven-year-old, three-bedroom rancher. There was no sign of any visitor, earthly or immortal.

"It was cold, very cold, when she passed by me," Loretta said. "I got goose bumps. I got up and turned every light on in the house. She just kept walking, with her arms down at her side. I looked everywhere. I was so scared, I thought of going to the neighbors, but I didn't know anybody."

When the realization of what had happened registered, she grabbed for the phone and called her husband.

While waiting for Henry to return home, Loretta sat on the living room couch, rocking Eric. As her eyes kept searching the walls and doorways, she noted there wasn't a room or area of her home that hadn't, in some way, hosted a frightening visit or unexplainable signal from the beyond.

The thoughts started to come in flashes: the sounds, the moving objects, the shadowy figures, the "Mean Old Man."

But, before she became overwhelmed, Loretta paused, to gain control, to force her memories into some sort of focused, organized pattern.

They had moved into the one-level home about two years before. Prior to when Eric was born.

Beaver Brook Crest was a new community—located on county farmland between Routes 40 and 9—not far from historic Olde New Castle, Delaware.

Spirits weren't supposed to be in new houses, Loretta told herself the first night they arrived. She recalled thinking that because things started happening on their first night in the house.

She and Henry were exhausted from moving all the boxes and furniture. They ended up falling asleep atop an inflatable mattress on the living room floor. The kitchen was around the corner.

At three in the morning, they both were awakened by the sound of all the kitchen cabinet doors being slammed and opened several times. It initially sounded like gunshots going off. But, after it stopped a few minutes later, Loretta and Henry imagined they had been dreaming a similar dream. They attributed their runaway imaginations to their exhaustion from moving in.

Since Henry's job kept him on the road, Loretta spent a lot of time alone. One evening, while waiting for good friend to visit, Loretta heard a knocking at the living room door.

When she opened the door, there was no one in sight. Because of the length of her driveway, she knew no one could have gotten away in such a short amount of time.

A week later, while asleep on the couch, Loretta said she felt someone shake her, as if to wake her up. Then, she added, the unseen thing grabbed her very hard on the shoulders, with ice cold hands.

"I was so sure that someone had been there," Loretta said, "that I took a mirror and checked my arms and shoulders for fingerprint impressions. I told my husband, but he didn't believe me. He always thinks there must be some explanation for everything. He just kept telling me I'm crazy.

"He said he never saw anything. I told him I guess the ghosts just seem to go for the women."

During another evening, she ran out of her bedroom searching for the source of the noises that were coming from the living room.

"It sounded like a courtroom," Loretta said. "There were men talking, a gavel being hit against another piece of wood. There was a clanging and women laughing. A whole group of people talking at the same time.

"But, when I came into the room, everything stopped completely. It was just like you came in on a bunch of people who had been talking about you and they all stopped cold, and at the same time. But it didn't really bother me. I've had stuff like this happen to me my whole life. But all this really bothers my husband. He doesn't even like to talk about it."

Perhaps the strangest series of incidents were associated with the "Old Mean Man" who would talk to Eric.

"He would tell me," said Loretta, "the Mean Man told me to get out of the bedroom. Eventually, Eric wouldn't sleep in there."

After Eric started complaining about the Mean Man pinching him, Loretta found marks and bruises on the child's body.

"He'd go right up to an area of the room and point at something he could see, but I couldn't," Loretta said. "Then Eric would turn to me and say: 'Tell the Mean Man to go away, Mommy.' On one occasion, when Eric was asleep in his bed, the Mean Man had pushed the boy's body against the wall of the room. He then had the back of Eric's head, moving in circles, against the lower portions of the boy's bedroom wall. You could see something, like a hand, was pressing into Eric's face. I grabbed him and we both slept in the living room."

Eric described the Mean Man as old, bald on top and with a large clump of hair on the back of his neck.

Eventually, Loretta said she started talking to the ghosts, often telling them to go away when she was too busy to be annoyed by their pranks.

Much of what they did seemed to be part of an effort to get her attention.

Loretta saw her couch cushions move and shift when no one was sitting on them. She also heard the furniture make distinctive squeaks when no one, including the dog, was near that particular piece of furniture.

When a heavy Christmas decoration floated five feet into the middle of the room from its resting place on the mantel of the fireplace, Loretta said she had reached her limit.

"I screamed, 'Leave me alone!' I was really upset," she recalled, then laughing, she added, "They left me alone for six months."

The cold areas of the house and sounds of shattering glass came occasionally. There also was the frequent smell of roses, even in winter.

"That smell was very heavy," Loretta said, "and it was accompanied by that feeling of coldness. You also always felt like someone was watching you. You never felt alone in that house."

One day, while washing clothes at the laundry area beside the kitchen, Loretta turned and looked down to her side. She was expecting to see Eric. Instead, it was the figure of a very young girl, who smiled, turned and skipped away.

"I knew it was them," she said. "They were trying to let me know they were back. I kept that one story to myself for quite a long time. I knew nobody would believe me."

One of the ghosts would call out "Psst!" trying to get her attention, then follow up with "Loretta!"

"I got so used to it. I just ignored it all. I knew they were trying to talk to me, but I didn't care.

"One night. It was late. I looked out the sliding glass doors at the back of the house and there was a pair of men's work boots, black and real worn out. The tips of the toes were curled up and scuffed. And there was a pair of gray pants, leading up into the darkness. They were the same color as that woman's dress. My husband told me he saw the old woman, late one night, passing down the hall. He thought it was me until he saw me in bed sleeping.

"That's when I decided there were two ghosts there," Loretta said. " I didn't count the little girl, since I only saw her one time."

Loretta talked to a few nearby neighbors. None of them admitted having anything strange occur in their homes.

She went to the county office to find out who had owned the land, but had no success. Someone told her to check the deeds in the courthouse, but she didn't understand the confusing procedures. Being from the area, she recalled that the site of her new home was very close to where the main farmhouse building had stood. She remembered it being all overgrown and damaged from years of neglect and being vacant.

From talking to old timers and listening to pieces of gossip, Loretta discovered an interesting story that offered explanations for a few of her experiences.

It was said that when the wife of the old farmer who owned the land died, he fell into a deep state of depression.

When the relatives arrived to view her body, he had his dead wife laid out in her bedroom, which was decorated with wallpaper featuring small pink roses and thin pink stripes.

Around the body and all over her bed were hundreds of fresh pink roses. The smell, they say, filled the entire house.

But, the story continues, he was so stricken with grief, that he couldn't bear to put her body into the ground. Instead, he bricked up the windows and doorway, sealing up her dead body in her rose decorated bedroom.

The ghosts of the farmer and his wife, Loretta suggested, may still be walking the site of their old homestead, unable to find their proper state of rest.

Interesting as that story may seem, there is one more aspect of Loretta's tale worth mentioning.

When she and her family moved out of the home, it was bought by Loretta's brother and sister-in-law. The new residents immediately made it very clear to Loretta that they never wanted to talk about her ghosts or any unexplained happenings.

Loretta is careful not to bring up anything about the past, or ask any questions of her relatives about present conditions in her old house.

"However," Loretta said, "they did tell me they've had all of their pots and pans swept off the kitchen counter. But they said it was the wind. And their little daughter refuses to sleep in her bedroom, the same one where Eric had frequent visits from the Mean Man."

Chaffee, the Friendly Ghost

About a half-dozen miles south of North East, Maryland, stands Hart's Chapel. It's a small, white wooden building. Its double front doors overlook the peaceful farmland that inclines downhill toward the shore of the Elk River.

In August 1777, the area was quite busy as the landing point for the more than 16,000 British troops and 4,000 Hessians in 300 ships who had arrived from New York. They were on their way to capture Philadelphia, battle General George Washington and crush the American revolt.

No one will ever know all the horrors of that war, just as the facts about the death and accidents that occurred during the British landings on that Maryland shoreline will remain secrets buried by time. But today, the quiet, secluded countryside along the river looks much like it did more than two centuries years ago.

In the late 1970s, almost exactly 200 years since the British invasion of Cecil County, Penny and Robert Thompson moved into a small white frame farmhouse on a large farm. They had no children when they arrived, and they stayed there only a few years. But the memories of what happened to them during their short stay will remain in their minds for the rest of their lives.

Since they lived in an old house, certain noises were expected. The natural causes were wind, varmints, the movement of household pets, the rustling of nearby trees and the settling of ancient timbers.

"The door to the cellar was always kept on a latch," Penny, an elementary school teacher, recalled. "Every night, after dark, I would hear a smash, a heavy crash against the thick wooden door, as if it were being kicked by a thick boot."

Penny was home alone a lot. Her husband, Robert, was a truck driver.

For weeks the sound persisted, usually only once a day. Penny said she eventually got used to it. Later, she noticed whenever she walked across a certain heating grate—the one that rested on the floor at the base of the stairway to the second floor—the metal would make a distinctive sound, almost a squeak.

When she was upstairs, Penny would hear the squeak, as if someone were walking across the grate. But she told herself it was the dog.

When she was downstairs, she would hear footsteps, as if someone was moving on the second floor. But she also attributed that noise to the family pet.

"But I started to notice that when the sounds happened, the dog was with me or nearby," she said. "It would happen in the daytime and at night, mostly at night. But it was never scary. We started saying, 'Oh, it must be the ghost!' Laughing about it. But the more we said it was the ghost, the more things seemed to happen. Almost as if the ghost was saying, 'Yes! It's me!' and it would walk around some more."

The couple noticed that their clocks, which had never worked or were always fast or slow, started to keep the correct time. One was a wind up clock; another ran by electricity; and a third was a quartz.

Wondering why all of their timepieces had suddenly started to work properly, Penny suggested it might have something to do with their ghost.

Robert thought his wife was crazy.

Until . . .

"Until the day I came down from the second floor bedroom and found my pocket watch on the dining room table," Robert said.

Penny had given Robert the watch as a gift several years before, but it never functioned well and couldn't be repaired. She kept it in the bottom of one of her dresser drawers, deep in her jewelry box.

"It was sitting on the dining room table," Robert recalled, "and it was working! Giving perfect time. And we said the ghost must have done it."

The spirit's presence became common knowledge among the Thompsons' relatives and visiting friends. At times, the spirit would move the rocking chair, once even tossing Penny toward the floor when she and several girlfriends were involved in a lengthy conversation where the topic happened to be man bashing in general terms.

On another occasion, the ghost turned up the volume dial on the stereo receiver.

When the Thompsons had their first child, Tommy, the baby boy always seemed relaxed, as if it was being tended by some unseen babysitter. When he became older and began to talk, Tommy told his parents, "Read louder to me, Daddy. So my friend can hear."

When Robert asked about the friend, the child said it was listening from the top of the stairs, or sitting in a nearby apple tree.

During a walk through the meadow toward the riverbank, Tommy said, "Daddy, don't walk so fast. My friend can't keep up with you."

The family ghost was tagging along for the trail walk.

It was during a breakfast conversation when the focus turned to the ghost. As discussion began to center on what its name might be, Tommy kept saying, what sounded to Penny and Robert, like "coffee."

His mother told him he was too young, at only two-and-a-half, to drink coffee.

When he repeated the word several more times, his parents realized the boy was saying "Chaffee."

Chaffee, they decided, was apparently the name of the Thompson' permanent unearthly house guest.

"We started calling him 'Chaffee,' " Penny said, "and we would joke and laugh about our having a ghost in the home."

During a parade held in Elkton, Maryland, the county seat, the Thompsons were on the sidelines, watching the marching bands, clowns and fire engines.

Suddenly, Tommy began shouting: "It's Chaffee! It's Chaffee!" as he pointed toward a unit of American Revolutionary War re-enactors who were marching proudly down Main Street in their Colonial era uniforms.

A few months later, Robert Thompson told the story of the family ghost to a friend who had attended Pennsylvania Military College. They explained why they thought he might be an old Colonial soldier. A few weeks later, the friend called back and said he had done some research.

The former military student said there was an officer on the American side during the Revolution who had been an aide to General Marquis de Lafayette. The Frenchman had accompanied General Washington when the American leader rode to Elkton to scout the British landing force in August 1777.

"The name of Lafayette's aide," Robert Thompson said, "was Choffee . . . and . . . he had been a watchmaker."

"We thought it all made sense," said Penny. "General Howe and the British landed here. So we had a feeling our ghost might be a soldier. When we heard that, we really thought we had a handle on who he was and we truly welcomed him as a member of the family."

A few years later, the Thompsons needed more room and decided to build a home, not too far away, on Old Elk Neck Road.

Since new tenants were moving into the old farmhouse, they had to leave before their new home was completed. The Thompsons set up a trailer in the woods, beside their construction site and lived there for several months.

Someone told them if they had a large empty box the ghost might jump inside and move with them.

They tried the suggestion, but with no result.

Things were very quiet at the new home site. Apparently, Chaffee did not go with them.

After several months, Penny decided to go back to the farm and visit a friend who lived in another house on the property. As she got ready to return to her new home, Penny couldn't resist knocking on the door of the building where she had lived.

When she tried to ask the tenant about Chaffee, the new resident's curt reply indicated that she did not want to hear about any ghost, friendly or not.

Penny returned to her cramped trailer a bit depressed.

Most of her possessions had been put into storage and were awaiting their resurrection when the new house was completed.

She looked up, above the entrance that led from the kitchen area to the trailer's small living room. On the wall, above the doorway was her favorite clock, broken during the move and now with only a single hour hand. The clock's minute hand had been lost in the moving boxes or during packing.

Later that night, as Penny was preparing to take the glass lid off a birthday cake she had baked for her son's party, she looked down at the top of the cake, gasped, then let out a brief scream.

There, gently resting on the top of the swirled, decorative icing leaves, was a thin, delicate gold hand—from a clock.

Penny's favorite clock.

The metal sliver that had been lost for months, somehow had found its way onto the cake that was enclosed within the closed glass cover.

"Chaffee's back!" she shouted. There was happiness in her voice.

Her husband ran over to see what had caused her exclamation of joy. "Chaffee!' he said, excitedly.

"Chaffee! We'd love you to stay!' Penny shouted, as her husband added his agreement.

But that apparently was his last visit. His last appearance. His final going away gift.

The Thompsons said their clocks still don't keep the correct time, except for one, Penny's favorite clock that will always have a special place on the living room wall.

The Ghosts of Ashley Manor

What I'm going to tell you is a true story. It happened in Cecil County, only a few years ago.

I write part time for a local paper, have done so for years. I was assigned a Halloween story, but my editor stressed that he wanted me to interview a family that lived with a ghost. After several calls to my sources in the real live ghost community, I secured a lead and set up an interview.

A week and a half before Halloween, when the leaves were turning bright colors and beginning to fall from the trees, I drove to Ashley Manor, then the home of Clayton and Caroline. They had moved to Cecil County about 10 years before and bought a three-story, 22-room, Federal-style mansion that had built in the early 1800s by a prominent county and state delegate.

Originally, the structure was surrounded by a plantation of a few hundred acres. Today it stands on a hill overlooking the shores of a county river—south of the Elk and north of the Sassafras—on a spit of land, called a neck by the locals, that reaches out toward the water like the longest finger of your hand.

From its white-fenced widow's walk at the top, you have a magnificent view of the upper reaches of the Chesapeake Bay. That's where the original owner would go to watch his ships come up the waterway toward Elkton and deliver cargoes of spices, fine cloth and slaves.

Upon my arrival, I was immediately impressed by the couple's distinctive attire. Clayton was wearing gleaming black boots, with his dark trousers tucked inside each leg. A dark, unbuttoned vest was atop his white, fluffy cuffed shirt that he wore opened at the collar.

Caroline, like her husband, was in her early 50s. She was dressed in a full-length, hooped skirt. On her fingers were several large-stoned rings, and an ornate, mother-of-pearl comb was affixed to the back section of her hair.

They had spent time and money restoring the mansion. Her early American antique plate and teapot collection was displayed on several walls of the study. His array of ancient weapons—from cap-and-ball pistols to flintlocks and pirate swords—decorated the walls of the large foyer. A good-sized bowl of musket balls rested on the top edge of an antique bureau.

To get my attention, they led me to a corner of the living room and carefully pulled out a glass cabinet door. It was coated with dust, but you could still see the ripples in the ancient glass, hand made more than a century before by an unknown craftsman.

The couple had planned to refinish the piece and place it back onto the bookcase of an old desk. It had rested in the back of a closet for five years for safekeeping.

In the top corner, boldly written in script and clearly readable in a fine layer of dust, were the words: "*Please help me.*"

They had my attention.

In the next three hours, while we all were seated under flickering candlelight around a large dining room table, the couple presented a succession of unusual occurrences that filled my two note pads.

There were the usual:

* Crashing noises in the middle of the night.
  (When everyone was asleep.)
* Footsteps walking the halls.
  (When only one person was home.)
* The pungent aroma of tobacco.

(Although no one in the house smoked.)

* The sweet smell of roses that filled the dining room. (In mid winter, when no flowers were in the house.)
* Cat footprints traveling up a hanging wall mirror and familiar animal scratchings outside their bedroom door. (The day after the family pet was killed in the roadway in front of the house.)
* Voices calling out unfamiliar names.
* Conversations in an unknown language.
* Chilling, sinister laughs.

Soon after moving in, the couple was getting gas at an area station and the attendant said, "You must be the folks who moved into the haunted house!"

Clayton and Caroline laughed, thinking the man was referring to the home's sad, paint-chipped appearance.

Not so.

While unpacking, after Clayton had left for work and her two daughters were at school, Caroline heard footsteps walking back and forth in the second floor hallway. Eventually, the steady sound seemed to be coming toward her down the stairs.

Startled, she shouted out, half in fun, "I don't know who you are, but we're going to be living here together. So we might as well plan to all get along."

The footsteps stopped.

When she told Clayton, who was a chemist by profession, he talked to her calmly, trying to explain what had "possibly" occurred rationally, just as any 20th-century scientist would. Then he told his wife, "Don't go telling this nonsense to anyone else. You don't want them to come and put you away!"

She listened patiently and finally replied, "Fine. You think I'm crazy. Just wait. You'll get yours one day."

It didn't take long until he did.

We got up from the table. It was quiet, dark outside by now, and Clayton led me into their cellar, a dirt floored area with several rooms but only one doorway that served as both the entrance and exit. It was where he spent a lot of time, working on items that were needed to repair the house.

He pointed to a locked door. Triple locked, with a small opening—like a slot similar to a jailer's window. It could be slid back so you could look inside and pass things through it.

"We don't go in there," he said, pointing to the triple locked room. "Try not to open it often. They say that was the 'Screaming Room,' where they punished the bad slaves. . . . "

I waited for more.

"Late one night, a black cloaked figure was standing at the entrance doorway, blocking my way out," Clayton recalled. "It just looked at me. It was all fuzzy, cloudy, but it had the most piercing green and red eyes. The figure seemed to be moving, floating toward me, and those eyes, they actually bore right into my chest. The heat was unbearable. I thought I couldn't breathe. Then, just as I was going to pass out, the cloaked figure drifted backwards, then turned and floated sideways, through the slave room door and was gone. . . . I try not to spend too much time down here at night."

Walking farther toward the rear of the cellar, my host pointed to a distinct outline of what seemed to be a pit, about five-foot square. It had notches on either side, where a log or piece of wood could be placed across. He guessed the hole was more than 12 feet deep.

I assumed it was a well.

"That's what I thought, too," Clayton replied. He turned and picked up a metal tray full of small items he had pulled from the pit. There were buttons, broken pottery, material from a frayed black collar, a half dozen arrowheads, several musket balls, and what he guessed were small slivers of some kind of bone.

Standing over the dark pit in the dimly lit cellar, Clayton recalled a yard sale they had held on the front lawn. It was about a year after moving in, and they had not told anyone about their strange experiences.

A man was buying some small trinket and the customer referred to the spooky looks of the house.

"I guess you got a lot of ghosts in there," he said, laughing.

Taken off guard, Clayton nervously replied, "Oh, we might have one or two."

"More than that," came a sharp voice from off to the side.

Clayton turned, forgot about the man and moved to the older woman who had offered the information.

She was well dressed, in a suit and expensive boots. "What can you tell me? Please?" Clayton asked her.

The woman kept walking, ignoring his questions. Suddenly she turned, pointed a finger directly toward the house, and said, "That pit in your cellar. . . ."

"Yes?" Clayton replied.

Her voice was a hoarse whisper. "They used to hang disobedient slaves down there."

Before he could ask her more, she abruptly turned to walk away. At the same time someone called out to purchase a few items. By the time Clayton had an opportunity to look again, the woman had disappeared. No car drove off. No one picked her up. She just vanished.

Frantic, Caroline and Clayton got in touch with the former owners. They were farmers, both over 80 years old. They had lived in the old mansion for more than 40 years. Seated around the dining room table, the new owners discovered that the former residents had many of the same experiences.

The former owners said they didn't tell anyone what was happening to them because they thought their kids might put them away. Since they were selling, they were afraid to say anything because it might mess up any sale.

To a certain degree, Clayton and Caroline were happy with the news, for, at times, they thought they had been going slowly insane. "We were afraid to tell our friends and new neighbors too much," Clayton said. "We thought they'd think they were crazy, and next thing you know, somebody for sure would come and try to put us away."

The two couples talked for hours about the ghostly events in their common home.

All four nodded in agreement about the sound of the penny that seemed to drop out of thin air and land in the darkness. It would make repeated whirling sounds for more than an hour in their bedroom during the earliest hours of the morning.

They talked about the night a table, holding crystal figurines, had been turned upside down. But all the small pieces of crystal were standing upright and unharmed on the floor beside the table.

Clayton and Caroline recalled the evening, just before midnight, when they both were reading in bed. Simultaneously, they stared in silence as a three-foot length of bright yellow ribbon floated across the room—from left to right—and disappeared into the opposite wall.

The older couple had a possible explanation for that strong smell of winter roses, that seemed as if it was being pumped into the dining room. They said years ago dead bodies had been laid out in the room, when it had been used as a parlor, during wakes just before burials.

Interestingly, Caroline said after that long evening of comparing experiences she felt a lot better about their historic home.

"Besides," she added, "even when you are home by yourself, you never feel like you're alone."

I asked the couple the obvious questions: "Why do you stay?" and "Why don't you move away?"

They had several reasons. First, it had been their home for more than 10 years. They had restored it themselves and it was their way of preserving a part of American history that was falling into ruin and neglect.

They also wanted to leave something of value and of themselves to their children. (Incidentally, the two girls who each lived in the home for a portion of time, will not even come back for a short visit. They meet their parents at a nearby restaurant .)

Caroline said they had considered bringing in a psychic, and maybe even asking a priest to come bless the home. Someone suggested both of those approaches might rid the place of the spirits.

After long consideration, Clayton and Caroline decided not to take any action. They decided that perhaps the spirits they currently had were somewhat benevolent and maybe even protective of them. They all seemed to get along somewhat.

If the priest or psychic drove them off, just maybe, something else would come in and take their place. They asked themselves: "What if the spirits that they knew were actually protecting them from a patiently waiting evil force that could be much worse?"

As I walked out the door, they thanked me for coming and for being so patient.

I was invited back, and was told that I could bring my wife. They didn't get many visitors, Caroline said.

I agreed to try to stop by, during the day, of course. Everyone offered a nervous, but understanding, laugh.

Clayton shook my hand and then took a musket ball from his pocket.

"It's just a little something I found on the grounds," he said. He wanted me to have it as a souvenir. I tried to refuse, but he insisted, pressing it into my palm.

They said it was a nice evening, and I had been kind to listen for so long.

They waved from the porch.

I looked back at them, thinking to myself: *There are two poor souls living a dilemma.*

As I drove home, I kept looking in the rear view mirror, almost expecting to see a ghostly traveling companion. Three weeks earlier I had interviewed several ghost hunters. I remembered their comment that it is possible to pick up a ghost from a haunted house if it decided to go with you and take up residence in a new site.

I do recall that the car was unusually cold, even the heater didn't do its normal job.

It was late when I arrived home. I emptied my pockets, took out the musket ball and placed it next to my wallet, on a small, gold dish resting on my bureau.

I stared at the round, pitted metal for a second, wondering where it had been, who had made it, what body it might have passed through and in what battle of what war it might have been used.

The next morning, I was rushing to get ready to run out the door for work. As I grabbed for my keys and wallet, I paused, noticing that my musket ball was gone.

I crawled onto the floor, peeked under the bed. Looked on my desk. Couldn't keep searching, it was getting late.

I rushed to the parking lot.

Unlocking my car door, I paused. Stopped.

The discolored ball was there, resting in the center of my driver's seat.

Could I have dropped it?

NO.

I was sure.

Was I, really sure?

Yes.

A chill passed throughout my body.

I picked up the small circle of iron and put it inside my coat pocket.

Adjusting my rear view mirror, I focused on the frost covering the back window of the car. Suddenly, I froze as the reflection in the mirror met my eyes, drawing my attention to the words carefully written in smooth script across the back windshield of my car:

"*Please help me!*"

Screaming, I ran from the car, dashed to the back of the parked vehicle.

But there was nothing there. No marks on the glass.

Nothing at all.

The window was clear. Smooth. Covered with a thin layer of frost.

But I saw it. I know I had read the same words that I had seen the night before on the dusty glass of the antique bookcase door.

Nothing would ever make me think or believe otherwise.

Jumping into the car, I drove, not to work, but in the opposite direction, far below the Chesapeake & Delaware Canal.

I headed south, until I turned west on a narrow road that raced off toward the wetlands and the marshes of the quiet part of the county.

Pushing the car to its limits down the narrow road, I skidded to a stop. I had reached the driveway of the home at which I had spent so many hours to the night before.

No one was out and about.

It was still early, quiet.

You could hear the birds, still see frost from your breath.

I pulled out the musket ball, held it tight and threw it hard and far, into the yard in the direction of the outside cellar entrance of Clayton and Caroline's Federal mansion known as Ashley Manor.

I hoped that was enough.

It was all I could think of. All I had that whatever it was could possible ever want from me.

Later, that very night, I wrote the story. Sent it into my editor.

They printed it exactly as I had written it.

But I left out the part at the end, the section about the musket ball that I just shared with you.

After all, I didn't want anyone to think I was crazy, or try to put me away.

—*Ed Okonowicz*

Visits from the Black Cat

Hollis Young is a big man, now in his 70s. He lives in Rock Hall, Maryland, not too far from the waters of the upper Chesapeake Bay. His voice reflects the sound of the Eastern Shore, the clipped talk of a waterman with a noticeable, but comfortable, blend of country and southern dialects.

He grew up in a house in Chestertown, in Kent County, Maryland. The wooden home was on High Street, across the way from the cemetery, not too far from the railroad tracks.

Hollis recalled, how as a young boy, he and his friends would play games in the graveyard. He laughed as he described how they would jump out from behind tombstones, carry lanterns behind the worn stone markers and even shake the smooth granite gravestones to catch the reflection from the streetlights and bounce the light through the rows of tombstones. They'd try anything that would scare passersby, Hollis said.

"We scared one boy so much," Hollis said, "the little fella would hit the railroad tracks, near the cemetery, and break out in a full run. An' wouldn't stop 'til he got clear home."

When asked to share any old ghost stories, Hollis talked a little bit about the headless dog that would appear in the farm areas of the county. But he selected a story told to him by his father, many, many years ago.

One night, Hollis' parents were sitting at the kitchen table, when his father asked, "When did we get us a black cat?"

"We ain't got no black cat," the mother said.

"Well, we sure must do," the father replied. " 'cause I just saw one go across the floor and walk into that pantry."

The couple got up and checked the small pantry, the whole kitchen, and all the rooms downstairs.

There was no black cat to be found.

Two days later, Hollis' grandfather, who lived in a house next door, died.

Two years later, the same couple was sitting at the same kitchen table. Just as occurred once before, a black cat walked across the floor and entered the pantry.

Hollis' father asked, "When did we get us a black cat?"

"We ain't got no black cat," said the mother.

"Well, we sure must do," the father replied. " 'cause I just saw one go across the floor and walk into that pantry."

The couple got up, as they had done two years earlier. Again they checked the pantry, the kitchen and all the rooms downstairs.

This time, as last, there was no black cat to be found.

The next day, Hollis' aunt, his father's sister, died of an accidental gunshot wound from a pistol, in the same house next door.

After the funeral, Hollis recalled his father say, "I hope I don't never see that black cat again."

Finally at Rest

Martin's encounter with the unusual did not occur on Delmarva, but rather in England more than 10 years ago. While a decade has passed, and an ocean separates the events from Martin physically, he did bring his intriguing memories back to the states, where they now remain with him in his Rehoboth Beach home.

An artist by profession, Martin was in his mid twenties in 1984, when he was living in Durrington, a moderate-sized village near the larger town of Worthing. His friends, Bert and Marilyn, had moved into an attractive English cottage and invited the artist to stay in a spare room. The couple had been in the home about three weeks when Martin arrived.

He recalled his room was nearly empty, an isolated straight back, wooden chair against one wall, a few boxes in a corner. Having no furniture that first night, Martin fell asleep on a small mattress that he had spread across the wooden floor.

"I woke up," he said, "and there was a guy sitting in a chair. I was looking up at him from my mattress on the floor. I checked the clock and rubbed my eyes, to be sure I was awake. It said one o'clock."

Martin took care to recall how the visitor was dressed and appeared. He said the figure had shoulder-length hair and was sitting in the chair. His legs were crossed and he was smoking a cigarette, a hand-rolled type. Being an artist, Martin took special note of the man's color scheme. It was all in shades of tan. An off-white shirt, a beige vest, darker slacks and tall brown boots.

"I remembered from somewhere that you are supposed to ask a ghostly figure why it is there, or who it wants. That's what I did," said Martin. "But the figure seemed to become agitated and upset. He snapped at me, said "This is a waste of time!' or 'You're wasting my time!' "

Martin turned his head away, just for a second, to check the clock. It said five after one. He knew he was still awake.

The young artist's mind was still trying to function. It didn't, couldn't understand why he could be wasting the vision's time. *What did he mean*? Martin asked himself.

But when he returned his gaze toward the visitor, only a second later, the figure had taken on an entirely different form. It had a shaved head and was wearing a uniform. It was a brown British army uniform, like the ones worn in World War II. But, during this transformation, the figure had become more agitated. By that time, it had become very angry looking.

"This really scared me," said Martin. "I took another look at the clock. It was ten after one in the morning. I had tried to keep my eyes on him, but he started to disappear. That's when I ran into Bert and Marilyn's room. She was already awake in their bed. I remember, she was sitting up, crying. And she shouted for me to tell her what was going on in my room. Apparently, she knew something had happened."

Into the darkness of the early English morning, the two new owners shared with Martin what had been happening during their first few weeks alone in the home. Mysterious footsteps, cracked plumbing pipes, problems with the electric outlets, a broken water heater and several items that had become lost later reappeared.

In addition to all the usual annoying signs that gave the impression an unearthly visitor resided in their midst, there was another series of unexplainable incidents.

Each night, Bert would lock the padlock on the shed that stood in the yard behind the house. But each morning, the shed padlock would be open and the lock's hook was dangling from the hasp. There were no indications of forced entry. It was as if someone has a key. But Bert had the keys in his possession since he only recently had bought the lock.

In addition, the previous owner had left behind a large number of family photographs on shelves in the shed. Several times, Bert said he would find several old, faded photographs had been pulled from among the hundreds in the stacks. The selected pictures—of a young man and woman—would be resting on the flat workbench area, face up, in the shed.

Martin and Marilyn decided to seek an explanation, or some clues, by approaching an elderly woman who had lived for years in the home next door. She told them the previous owner was still alive, then in her late 80s, living in an area nursing home.

When Martin made the visit and explained where he now lived, the former owner, who was named Margaret, casually said, "Oh. I forgot to tell my brother I had moved."

"It was just a natural expression in her conversation," Martin recalled. "She said Robert, her bother, had been drafted into the army during World War II in England. But he didn't like the service. He was very uncomfortable, and he died during a German bombing raid over the area."

Martin recalled that Margaret said, since his death, Robert continued to visit her every two weeks. She started to become very upset when she realized he was still out there somewhere looking for her.

The older woman said Robert would never appear to anyone, unless he felt totally comfortable with them. You see, she explained to Martin, Robert was gay. But even in the 1940s, when homosexuality was kept very quiet in families, her brother was very confident about his sexual preference .

His sister apparently had accepted her brother's sexual inclination and was not bothered and did not speak about it as anything controversial. She also did not seem surprised that Robert had allowed himself to been seen by Martin.

I asked Martin if he was gay.

He said he was.

When Martin returned to Bert and Marilyn's home, he explained what he had learned. The couple took the news in mixed ways.

Like many who have lived with unexplained incidents, a discovery of some type of reason for their trouble was comforting news. However, the next step that sometimes occurred was a serious effort to get rid of the unwanted resident.

Knowing of Bert's plans to take action against the ghost, Martin tried to contact Robert, to talk to him and explain that his sister Margaret was elsewhere, but it did not work.

Bert, meanwhile, had decided to summons a local priest, who was asked to bless the house and exorcise the spirit.

Martin, who did not agree with the approach, took several photographs from the shed and placed them in the home, on the mantel and in several rooms. He continued to try to make contact with Robert, but without any positive results.

Bert persisted in his plan to call upon a priest for outside assistance.

Martin did not plan to be in the home at the time. He was leaving when the priest arrived and he witnessed the cleric turn to Bert and say: "You, sir, are not fooling anyone here. You are still a married man who is living in sin with this woman in this house!"

The truth of the accusation and the wonder of how the priest could have known, gave Martin the impression that things were going to get hot in his temporary home. It did not take long.

Ignoring the priest's prayers and blessing, Robert, who remained unseen, continued to work his mischief. The couple was remodeling the kitchen and got a permit from West Sussex government. They planned to extend the room out into the back yard and replace the original wall with a greenhouse-style, large section made of glass.

One day, the sound of shattering glass could be heard throughout the entire house. It was as if an explosion had occurred and all the windows were broken and shattered. Simultaneously, Martin, who was in an upstairs room and hadn't touched anything, looked down and saw his hands had broken out in cuts and thin red marks that were bleeding.

"I had been trying to talk to Robert, mentally, for some time," said Martin. "But I couldn't seem to get through. I could sense he was very upset, that he was lost, trapped. He had no way to locate his sister or find peace. I wanted to help, but it was getting too frightening there. I decided to leave. In fact, it became so bad that my friends also left. I heard Marilyn had to spend some time in a mental hospital."

Before he left the country, Martin made a trip back in the area. The lady who lived next door said Martin's friends had moved out of the home. She added that things were all right by that time. He said he knew she was talking about Robert.

"I think Robert and Margaret found each other," said Martin. "At least I hope they did. Maybe now they're at peace."

Welcome to the Family

Connie was not quite 20 years old when she found herself spending a lot of time away from her house. It could be shopping at the mall, going to the movies, even wandering through the aisles of the 24-hour supermarket on the outskirts of Newark, Delaware.

It wasn't because she was bored.

Far from it.

The truth is: Connie was afraid, afraid to stay alone in her family's home in Robscott Manor.

It was a relatively new bi-level. Built in the mid 1960s, in a prime location, within walking distance of Delaware Stadium where the Fightin' Blue Hens hosted their opponents each fall in the cozy college town.

But Connie wasn't concerned with football. She was more interested in making it through another day—or night— without being hassled by any of her home's several resident ghosts.

One was the old man with the dark sunken eyes and the receding hairline who floated through the "cold room" at the end of the upper floor hall.

Or it could be the invisible guest who would change channels on the television set, in the days before remote control.

Then there was the specter who liked to turn on the water faucets in the bathrooms to make the water run, and flush the toilets, again and again and again.

And how could she forget the rhythmic Indian sounds that caused several family members to suggest that the house was built atop an Indian burial ground.

It was during one of her all night visits to the local supermarket that Connie met Bob Stacatto. They struck up a conversation while he was at work stocking shelves.

"I didn't know what to think at first," he admitted. "It wasn't often that you'd meet someone who said they were afraid to go home because of a ghost. Crazy parents, strict rules, no place to live. Those were common and understandable reasons to be out late roaming around."

The two hit it off, started dating and, eventually, were married. Bob found he had become a member of something other than your run-of-the-mill, Ozzie and Harriett-type family, especially when he stayed overnight in the house in Robscott Manor.

Among the couple's early marriage highlights were:

The newlywed's bed shaking violently in the middle of the night when both Connie and Bob were asleep.

Feeling some invisible person, or thing, sit down on the foot of the mattress, between the sleeping couple. It would then, slowly move between them, into the bed, putting enough pressure on the bed so that Connie and Bob would roll toward each other in the center of the mattress.

Friends who visited the couple commented to them on the sounds of heavy breathing. Other guests were a little bothered when they saw the walls move. Some complained about being pushed and having their hair pulled. One became very upset when a blanket she was sleeping under moved up past her chest and started wrapping itself tightly around her neck.

Bob's cousin Mark was visiting the Robscott Home one night. In the midst of a conversation, he suddenly stopped talking. Everyone waited for him to continue, but he was speechless. The other guests stared at him, with his mouth frozen open, as his eyes were riveted at the steps that led to the hallway with the "cold room."

Mark later said he watched a long procession of people—all surrounded by a fuzzy, green glow—floating up the stairs.

When Connie and Bob moved into Newark's Kimberton Apartments, they were sure they had left the wife's family spirits behind.

Not so.

When they opened their third floor apartment's door one evening, they heard the deafening sound of Indian chanting.

"It was coming from the living room. It was so loud we couldn't stay," Bob recalled. "But we couldn't go to her parents house. That was haunted. So we went to my parent's house and made up a story, that we didn't have any electric or heat or something."

After they returned the unusual events continued.

While talking on the phone in the kitchen, one would hear the sound of the phone receiver in the bedroom being lifted. But when either of them ran into the other room to check, the bedroom phone was resting on the hook, as it should have been.

But . . . the cord was swaying back and forth.

Bob's cousin Mark stayed with them a few times, but never for an extended period.

During his first visit, Mark asked Bob the name of the old man who was walking across the apartment hall from the bathroom to the bedroom.

"Oh. That's only our ghost," Bob replied, jokingly.

On different occasions, entire sets of towels, diapers, silverware, ashtrays and cups would disappear from the apartment. Then, Connie said, in a few days, they would appear again—as many as a dozen of each—and they would be neatly stacked, in various areas of the apartment.

After a time, the couple considered the disappearing pattern a routine part of their married life.

Bob laughed as he described what he still considers the most embarrassing incident in his life.

He and Connie were awakened in their apartment bedroom by the sound of crashing and breakage coming from their living room, downstairs.

Fearing for their safety, they pushed a heavy dresser bureau against their bedroom door and dialed 911. While Connie spoke to the police dispatcher, Bob was shouting for the robbers to leave, telling them he had a gun and that the police were on the way.

"It sounded like there were two or three people outside the door ransacking the place," said Connie. "We were sure they were breaking everything in the apartment."

When the dispatcher on the phone told Connie the police had arrived and they were outside the Stacattos' apartment door, Bob pulled the dresser back and walked out into the hall.

They had been listening to the racket for 15 or 20 minutes.

As he approached the living room, the noise stopped.

The police were beating on the door.

Bob had to undo three locks—the door handle, the deadbolt and the security chain.

"Nothing was touched," Bob said. "It was embarrassing. But it all happened, just the way we said it did."

The police left and were not pleased with Bob and Connie's ghostly explanation.

The strange things continued after their daughter Monica was born. Connie recalled how she and Bob would be sitting in the kitchen and hear the wind up mobile, that dangled above the crib, turn on and be playing in Monica's room.

At first they thought it was caused by the baby shaking the crib and the spring in the mobile being jarred by the movement. One night they listened through the door. They could hear the music and the sound of their baby laughing, as if being amused by a babysitter.

Bob quietly grabbed the handle and shoved open the door.

Inside there was nothing. Absolutely no sound. No movement.

The room was dark. The mobile was still and the baby was asleep.

Over and over it happened.

Bob said when he heard the music and laughter, he would crawl to the baby's door, twist the knob—so it would not click or get caught in the lock—and spring the door open.

Always the same. Nothing.

But for all the strange moments they shared in the several places they lived, it was Connie's days growing up at the Robscott Manor home that provided her most vivid and frightening memories.

It was very dark..at the end of a double date, early in the morning one weekend, when Bob and Connie drove back to her family's home. With them were Connie's brother, Freddie, and his new girlfriend.

Realizing he had forgotten his key, Freddie decided to climb in through one of the lower level windows. They were easy to access being even with the front lawn.

After he got inside and was walking through the dark basement area to find a light, Freddie said his dog was literally thrown at him through the air. The animal struck his chest with such force that it knocked him over. Then, he said, something he could not describe picked him up and pushed him against the wall.

His girlfriend, meanwhile, had been peering into the house through another low window and started screaming.

"She was totally hysterical," said Bob. "She said what she saw was the most hideous, gross thing that you could ever imagine. She said she wouldn't be able to describe what she saw. I thought we were going to have to lock her up and put her away. I know one thing, none of us never saw that girl again."

Now living a much less exciting life in a small home outside Elkton, Maryland, Connie admitted she still occasionally has paranormal experiences. None, she added with a smile, approach the intensity of her earlier contacts with the horrific.

Not surprisingly, flashes of curiosity about her family's former home in Robscott Manor occasionally enter her mind.

"I saw the first people who bought it after our family left when they were having a yard sale one weekend," said Connie. "I went there and walked up to the lady and started to ask her questions about the house. But she cut me off. Said she did not want to talk about it."

Connie noticed that family didn't live there too long, and the house was sold quickly, within about two years.

"I wrote a letter to the next owners," Connie said.

She sealed the envelope and had her husband deliver it.

Bob knocked on the door and asked the newest owner to give the note to his wife.

"Before I could tell him what it was about," Bob recalled, "he said, 'Nothing goes on here! Nothing happens here!' Then he shut the door and shouted, 'Go away!' "

Reflecting on their interesting life together, Bob said, "At first I thought she was a kook. I wondered: Who is this strange person I met. Now I look back on it and try to remember what it was like. We were really just teenagers. We thought it was cool, all this strange stuff. No one else had this happening to them.

"Now, I wonder how we lived through it, how we were able to handle it. I know I would never have stayed in those places or be able to do things the same way if they would happen again now."

Stay with us Again, Sam!

When Crystal Duffy and her family moved into their new, brick two-story home—in a isolated wooded area off Biggs Highway, near Bay View, Maryland—life seemed pleasant and simple. There were horse farms nearby, lots of rolling farmland, good community schools and easy access via nearby Interstate 95 to major shopping centers and work.

She had the best of both lives—rural charm and city conveniences, plus Sam the ghost.

Soon after Crystal unpacked the moving-in boxes, she started to notice little, unusual things.

"I would be sitting in the living room," she recalled, "and hear footsteps going up and down the hall. Lights would be switched on and off. And the basement door would open and close all by itself. I kept it to myself for about a month. I really thought I was going crazy."

Before they left for work one morning, Crystal and her husband were having breakfast. During the conversation, Ralph looked at his wife and softly said, "You know, I think there are some strange things going on here."

Delighted she wasn't losing her mind, Crystal and Ralph began comparing notes and discovered the same disturbing incidents had happened to both of them.

Mary, who was five at the time, entered the room and took a seat at the table. After a few moments of quiet, she added to the conversation by casually stating, "Oh. You two must mean Sam."

The parents looked a their youngest daughter, and simultaneously asked what she meant.

"Our ghost," she said. "His name is Sam."

After being pressed for information, Mary matter-of-factly shared what she knew. "Sam" was an American Indian—complete with bow, arrows, quill, feathers and pouch. He had been visiting the couple's youngest child at night in her room.

Mary said Sam—who she described as "Tall. He's a dad, and an Indian"—told her he used to live at the site where their home stood.

Crystal did some library research and determined that the Bay View area—in Cecil County north of North East, Maryland—had been a stopping site for migrating Indians hundreds of years ago.

Everyone in the family agreed that having Sam's presence as an explanation for the unexplainable events was positive.

The Indian's visits continued in the Bay View home, but with no regularity. Sometimes they would take place for a few days or weeks. Then, as suddenly as they had started, they would stop, Crystal explained.

There were, however, a few unusual occurrences that went beyond footsteps and closing doors. One morning, Crystal was asleep in bed and felt a body and steady breathing on the mattress next to her. But, when she happened to peek through her eyelid and look in the bathroom, she noticed her husband was awake, dressed and shaving for work.

"I could swear there was someone in bed with me," Crystal recalled. "I could hear the breathing, feel the pressure. It wasn't until I moved my arm, to rest it on what I had though was my husband's shoulder, that I was sure I was alone."

April, the family's oldest child, was both surprised and scared when she walked into the basement looking for a toy one summer afternoon. Sam was sitting in the middle of the room, on the floor, with his legs crossed Indian style. He said nothing and was still there, remaining in the same position, when April left the cellar heading for the safety of the first floor.

Ralph, who was working on a home repair project had lost a small, odd-sized washer that he needed to complete the job. He carefully searched the entire area where he had been working. Finding nothing, he had his wife and children do the same, and the whole family checked other parts of the house.

All with no success.

When he returned to the area where he had been working on the project, the missing part was clearly visible in the center of the floor, sitting in plain sight next to his tools.

"I think Sam just visited," was Ralph's immediate reaction.

Only once, said Crystal, did the benevolent spirit act in a frightening manner. John, who was 10 at the time, was staying home alone when the TV started turning itself on and off. Also, the VCR machine was going into its rewind and fast forward modes without anyone using the controls. There were footsteps all over the house, including the crawl space, located above the second floor, which is a very confined and tight area, too small for anyone to walk in.

John called his mother at work. She came home to find her son had taken refuge at a neighbor's home and was reluctant to re-enter his house.

Interestingly, Crystal said, that was the only time anyone was concerned.

"At that one house, where we lived with Sam," she said. "I had never been nervous. Staying home alone was not unpleasant. I was never fearful."

Because of demands associated with their jobs, three years after they arrived in Bay View, Crystal and her family moved to the Claymont area of adjacent Delaware. Her co-workers, knowing a bit about her resident ghost, gave Crystal a heavy cardboard box, with "For Sam" written on the sides.

Someone had told Crystal that a ghost might move with a family if they left an empty box overnight in the old house and then carried it to the new residence.

The family and some close friends joked as to whether their friendly Indian spirit would take advantage of the offer and head north with them.

"There was a big debate as to whether he would decide, or be able, to move with us," Crystal recalled.

The family made its relocation on a hot and humid Delmarva summer afternoon.

Late that Saturday night, upon waking from her sleep on the living room couch, Crystal thought she saw someone drifting down the main hall. Humorously, she joked, "Well, Sam's back, and it looks like he has a body."

The following Wednesday morning, Mary, again in casual conversation, said she saw Sam in the new house on Monday night. That was two days after the family had moved.

"He was wearing different clothes," the little girl said. "Maybe he found some new stuff in the attic."

What did he say to you? was the most obvious question.

"He said he might have to go back to the old house," Mary said. "Sam said he can't do anything for us anymore. He said he has to go back and do something with the new people who are at our old house."

That, however, didn't seem to be what the family wanted.

"I have always wondered if he would move with us," said Crystal. "I've never been able to decide what I really wanted. Part of me thinks we may be better off without him, and part of me thinks it's good that he's here and that he's watching over us. Especially after Mary said he was here. I like the feeling that he was here and that he was looking in on us. I guess only time and what happens here will tell."

Still in the Mansion

A large mansion rests in the wooded, eastern section of the Bellevue State Park, very close to the Philadelphia Pike, just north of Wilmington, Delaware.

In the 1850s, Hanson Robinson, a wealthy Philadelphia wool merchant built a Gothic style castle, named Woolton Hall, on the spacious estate. The land and buildings and Robinson's carriage collection were purchased in 1893 by William du Pont Sr. In 1928, it all was inherited by Willie du Pont Jr., a colorful, eccentric millionaire who loved horse racing, fox hunting, dressage and, later, tennis.

He built an indoor sporting complex, a full-size race track and added numerous stables. A major project was turning the three-story, dark stone castle into a replica of Montpelier, the Virginia home of President James and Dolley Madison, which his father had purchased in 1908. That Virginia home was where Willie spent much of his boyhood.

Because of his flamboyant style and unconventional behavior, some believe that, despite his death in 1965, Willie du Pont Jr. has never left his happy home.

Since the state purchased the property in 1976, its stables have been used for equestrian instruction. The mansion has become a well-known meeting site that hosts private receptions and for a time was a restaurant. The park's rolling meadows are used by joggers, riders and walkers, and its lawns host summer concert audiences.

Some park service personnel and visitors claim ghosts abound on the estate.

There are reports that:

* A woman in a white gown floats in the Horseshoe Gardens that face the front door of the Mansion.

* Regardless of how many times, and how many different people check to insure the light fixtures are turned off, someone or something flicks on at least one light before employees get to their cars in the parking lot. Many think it's Willie, letting them know he's still around.

* In some cases, horses that died in the stables are said to be buried in the woods of the estate. In 1964, a stable fire killed several thoroughbreds. Willie died the next year. Some claim they have heard the sound of phantom hoof beats in the indoor track and on the grounds in the darkness.

* At the end of a private reception late one evening, several young workers for a local caterer were cleaning in the Mansion. Since they had a breakfast event to prepare for early the next day, they received permission to stay overnight. They never made it until morning. Ghosts, they said, drove them out of the Mansion.

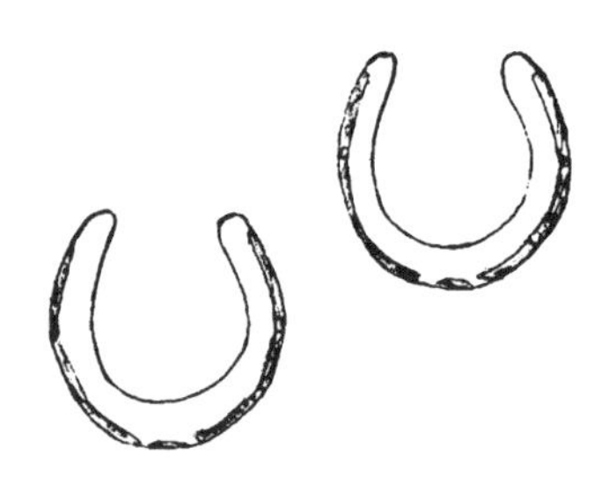

Headless Horseman of Welsh Tract Church

A silversmith named Paul Revere and two other patriots from Massachusetts made their famous rides on April 18, 1775, shouting: "The British are coming! The British are coming!"

Young men and husbands, from farms and villages, towns and cities, took up arms, left home and set out to fight the Redcoats and do their part to free America. The first major battles of the American Revolution took place at Lexington and Concord.

In July 1776 in Philadelphia, the Americans formally declared their independence. The young, disorganized Colonials were in full battle against the might of the powerful British Empire.

A year later, in late August 1777, the British planned to capture Philadelphia. But instead of going up the Delaware River, which they decided was too well defended and had treacherous shoals in its bay, they chose instead to sail into the Chesapeake Bay. The army, on 300 boats, traveled to the top of the Maryland bay and landed 16,000 British troops and 4,000 Hessian mercenaries. Men, horses and supplies entered land on the west bank of the Elk River, not far from Turkey Point in the area called Oldfield Point.

Washington, along with the young French General Marquis de Lafayette, came south from New Jersey and assembled the American troops in Wilmington, Delaware. The American commander then traveled into Elkton and stayed at Jacob Hollingsworth's

Tavern to observe the British movements. He later moved back to Newark, Delaware, and, during a thunderstorm, stayed at the Seth James farmhouse near Iron Hill.

The British marched east, to Summit, Delaware, then turned north, passing toward Lums Pond and headed straight for the small town of Newark.

Just as had occurred during Paul Revere's ride in Massachusetts, the call went out—from Newark and Wilmington to Chadds Ford and Christiana—"The British are coming! The British are coming!"

Young boys and fathers, uncles and sons, all grabbed their swords and muskets. Many kissed their girlfriends, mothers and wives and rode off to do battle with the British and fight beside General Washington.

One of the young men who had been waiting to answer the call of freedom was Charlie Miller, son of a grain merchant who had been supplying food to General Washington's troops for almost a year.

On more than one occasion, as they were delivering supplies under cover of darkness, both young Charlie and his father saw the great American general himself.

One night, General Washington noticed the two Millers unloading a wagon of grain. He was aware his poor American army had no money and could only offer a promise to pay. The general made it a point to thank the Millers personally, and he told them their country would always remember their kindness and how they demonstrated their faith in freedom.

Charles senior replied, "I'm doing it for my country, general. But it's also for my son. I want this war to be over before it takes young Charlie from me."

"I'm not afraid of the British, Father," Charlie said with vigor. "I'll kill as many Redcoats as I can for our country."

General Washington put his arm on the young man's shoulder. "You do your part in your own way, Charlie. Right now, bringing food for our men is your way of fighting. If the day ever comes, I know you'll be there, right beside me and my men, and you'll be brave and ready."

In August 1777, Charlie's time had come.

Then 16 years old, the boy mounted his family's white horse at their farm north of Wilmington. He took his sword and his father's musket, hugged his mother and promised to return. Riding off, he headed southwest toward Newark.

The British were moving at will throughout the area. The colonials tried to defend themselves, but on all sides they were outnumbered.

On Sept. 3, at Cooch's Bridge, a small creek crossing south of Newark, the Stars and Stripes flag was used in battle for the first time. But it had to be carried in retreat as the British and their German allies came in waves.

The Americans shot at the advancing enemy from behind trees and rocks, from dry gullies and streams.

Redcoats littered the Delaware summer fields and Americans in blue and white fell in the woods and forests. Small battles peppered the upper Delaware region. Each side moving slowly. But the British steadily gained the ground.

Charlie Miller was with a group who were defending the irregular stone walls surrounding Welsh Tract Church.

Few American volunteers had horses, most were poor foot soldiers. There were only about 30 Colonial fighters in the immediate area. Suddenly, a cannonball hit the ground and the few horses and men scattered. Dry dirt flew high into the air. The metal from the cannonballs shattered several gravestones and caused the defenders to shout in fear and confusion.

The British were coming, and their advancing small rifle fire peppered holes in the cemetery wall and marked the brick of the small square church.

Charlie, trying to stop his horse from running off, mounted his white steed. Then, upon turning to face the enemy, he was immediately hit, directly in the head, by a British cannonball.

The force of the hot, black projectile took off his head and continued on its journey, finally smashing into the center of the west wall of the church.

The beheaded American's friends, upon seeing what had happened, screamed and ran off in retreat. Amidst the bedlam, Charlie Miller's white horse, with its headless soldier, rode off into the woods.

He was never seen again.

At least that's what some people say.

On September 8, the British left Newark and headed for Chadds Ford, Pennsylvania. There, on September 11, the British and American armies would meet in the famous Battle of the Brandywine—named after the scenic river that flows though lower Pennsylvania and upper Delaware. Some say it was the largest battle of the Revolutionary War.

On the evening before that fight, General Washington was walking from his headquarters, a stone farmhouse not far from the Delaware border inside Pennsylvania. The American leader was headed toward the tents where his men slept. He often went out to speak to his soldiers, to talk to them about their homes and families. They would share their dreams and discuss what they planned to do after the war was won.

The general was tall, walked erect. His figure was well known, especially to the two British snipers who were hidden in the darkness of the nearby Pennsylvania woods.

Slowly, carefully, quietly, they aimed their muskets at the American hero. By killing the Colonial army leader, they knew they would win the war for England. The Americans would be lost, confused. They would have no leadership and they would surrender quickly.

The two Redcoats cocked the hammers of their muskets, took steady aim.

The General was so close. It was a sure shot.

No way they could miss.

Suddenly, General Washington stopped. For no apparent reason that anyone could see.

Then it appeared. Riding straight for the general, as if to run him down, was a large white horse.

It came out of nowhere, from the dark, tree shadows of the cool September night.

The horse seemed to pass directly through the American general's body. George Washington stared at the rider, a headless figure erect in the saddle, who was charging swiftly for the nearby wood line.

The two British marksmen changed their aim. Instinct made them fire at the threatening figure on the horse that was only 15 feet away.

Both shots hit their marks, ripping directly into the rider's chest.

But the blue coated ghost and its charging white horse did not stop. The figure was upon them, sword drawn.

A voice materialized from no seen source.

The angry sound bellowed deep from the hollow opening of the rider's open neck.

"I WAAAANT MYYYYY HEEEAAAAD!!!!"

The growl shattered the silence of the black countryside and turned the blood of those who heard it into ice.

"I WAAAANT MYYYYY HEEEAAAAD!!!!" it repeated.

The phantom rider never paused, his horse did not slacken its breakneck pace.

With one flashing sweep of his razor-sharp sword, the ghost of Charlie Miller claimed the heads of the two British marksmen as his personal prizes of war.

Despite their frantic efforts to reach the safety of the wood line, the snipers, like many of their comrades, were doomed.

General Washington and a handful of stunned troops stood in silence. For just as suddenly as he appeared, the specter vanished—horse and headless rider—in the darkness and mist, heading for the banks of the Brandywine.

During the next day, at the Battle of the Brandywine, there are those, both British and American, who swear they saw a headless rider on a white horse. He was seen riding down the British lines, appearing amidst the smoke of the battle, chopping off heads of the enemy, especially those manning the cannons.

He was shouting: "I WAAANT MYYYY HEEEAAAAD!!!"

The spirit also appeared later that winter, at Valley Forge. Although there was no major battle fought during that frozen encampment, the headless rider seemed to be scouting the edges of the camp. Working, they say, more as a sentry and guard, to protect the weary Americans from harm.

Several heads, believed to be those of British soldiers who had gotten too close to the American campsite, were discovered by area residents in the spring, after the ice and snow had thawed.

There are people, to this day, who say a lone horse and figure still ride the backroads of Newark, near Washington's Chadds Ford Headquarters and along the narrow banks of the Brandywine Creek.

It is recommended that those who walk in the evening shadows of the woods and hollows, keep off the chill with a coat or sweater of Colonial Blue.

If that is not possible, one should avoid wearing any color that comes close to bright, British Red.

For Charlie Miller, the Headless Horseman of Welsh Tract Church, still displays his dislike for the British in a dramatic and very permanent way.

On the west side of Welsh Tract Church, between the two first floor windows, visitors can still see the patched brickwork, which covers damage caused by the British cannonball.

Blackbeard's Pirate Treasure

In the area of northern Delaware known as Blackbird—located north of Smyrna and east of Townsend—there are tales of chests filled with gold and treasure that were hidden centuries ago by the famous pirate Edward Teach, better known as Blackbeard. The famous figure of legend and lore is believed to have visited the Blackbird Creek area in 1717 and early in 1718, and other sites along much of the Delaware Coast as well.

The area of Blackbird is named after the 18th-century swashbuckler, who was well known for his erratic behavior and 13 wives. Treasure hunters-have been searching the area for hundreds of years.

Some claim to have found evidence of decaying pirate forts, built of wood in the marshes. But, despite using metal detectors and aerial and satellite photography, no one has of yet publicly claimed the chests and sacks full of Blackbeard's captured gold and jewels. Many believe much of it still lies buried somewhere along the state's sandy coastline and marshy wetlands.

Blackbeard was a large man, with a beard that extended below his waist. To add to his bizarre, almost demonic, appearance, the pirate wore his beard in pigtails tied with ribbons, one in honor of each of his wives. To add a bit of theatrical drama to his already strange looks, he tied two, slow burning cannon fuses from either side of his face. When lit, they enveloped his head in a dark, foggy cloud. The pirate also would mix a dash of gunpowder in his rum and set it on fire, then smile at any onlookers as he drank down the flaming liquid.

In late 1718, near his hideout in a cove off Ocracoke Inlet in North Carolina, Blackbeard was shot five times and suffered nearly two dozen cuts in a sea battle with Lieutenant Robert Maynard of the Royal Navy. The officer, fearing Blackbeard might somehow come back to life, had the pirate's head cut off and hung it from a mast off the bow, then tossed the body overboard.

Legend says that Blackbeard's ghost, holding a lantern, is still searching for its head and roams the beaches of North Carolina as well as the wetlands of the Delaware and Chesapeake Bays. Unexplained flashing lights on the North Carolina shoreline are often referred to as Teach's Light.

Some experts say the well-known pirate will not rest until his treasure has been found by modern day hunters. Others, however, believe differently. They claim Blackbeard's ghost appears only when treasure seekers get too close to his booty, for the ghost of the pirate is standing watch to insure that his loot stays hidden and will remain only his forever.

About the Author

Ed Okonowicz, a Delaware native, is a freelance writer for local newspapers and magazines. Many of his feature articles have been about ghosts and spirits throughout the Delmarva Peninsula. He is employed as an editor and writer at the University of Delaware, where he earned a bachelor's degree in education and a master's degree in communication.

Also a professional storyteller, Ed is a member of the National Storytelling Association and several regional storytelling organizations. He presents programs at country inns, retirement homes, schools, libraries, public events, private gatherings, birthday parties, Elderhostels and theaters in the mid-Atlantic region.

He specializes in local legends and folklore of the Delaware and Chesapeake Bays, as well as topics related to the Eastern Shore of Maryland. He also writes and tells city stories, many based on his youth growing up in his family's neighborhood beer garden–Adolph's Cafe–in Wilmington. He tells tales about the unusual characters each of us meet in our everyday lives.

Ed presents beginning storytelling courses and also writing workshops based on his book *How to Conduct an Interview and Write an Original Story*.

About the Artist

Kathleen Burgoon Okonowicz, a watercolor artist and illustrator, is originally from Greenbelt, Maryland. She studied art in high school and college, and began focusing on realism and detail more recently under Geraldine McKeown. She enjoys taking things of the past and preserving them in her paintings.

Her first full-color, limited-edition print, *Special Places*, was released in January 1995. The painting features a stately stairway near the Brandywine River in Wilmington, Delaware.

A graduate of Salisbury State University, Kathleen earned her master's degree in professional writing from Towson State University. She is currently a marketing analyst at the International Reading Association in Newark, Delaware.

The couple resides in Fair Hill, Maryland.

Volume II

Opening the Door

13 more true-life Delmarva ghost tales and one peninsula legend.

$8.95

"Scary" Ed Okonowicz . . . the master of written fear—at least on the Delmarva Peninsula . . . has done it again.
WILMINGTON NEWS JOURNAL

96 pages 5 1/2 x 8 1/2 inches softcover ISBN 0-9643244-3-1

Volume III

Welcome Inn

Features true stories of unusual events in *haunted* inns, restaurants, and museums

$8.95

96 pages 5 1/2 x 8 1/2 inches softcover ISBN 0-9643244-4-X

Volume IV

In the Vestibule

Tales of suspense drift beyond the bays, to the Jersey shore, Philadelphia and Baltimore suburbs and, of course, back into Delmarva.

Coming in the Fall of 1996

I am constantly looking for more stories. If you have had a ghostly experience with an object or if you know of a haunted site that is accessible to the public, I would appreciate hearing from you. Please use the form on Page 58.

To order additional volumes, or to share an encounter or tale

To submit your personal experience for consideration, to purchase additional books or to be placed on our mailing list, please complete the form below.

Name ____

Address ____

City __________________________________ State _______

Zip Code ____

Phone Numbers ( ) _______________ ( ) _______________
Day Evening

_____I would like to be placed on the mailing list to receive the free *Spirits Speaks* newsletter and information of future volumes.

_____I have an experience I would like to share. Please call me.
(Each person who sends in a submission will be contacted. If your story is used, you will receive a free copy of the volume in which your experience appears.)

I would like to order the following books:

Quantity	Title	Price	Total
	Pulling Back the Curtain, Vol. I	$8.95	
	Opening the Door, Vol. II	$8.95	
	Welcome Inn, Vol. III	$8.95	
	Stairway over the Brandywine, A Love Story	$5.00	
		Shipping	
		Total	

Please include $1.50 postage for the first book, and 50 cents for each additional book.

Send to: Ed Okonowicz
1386 Fair Hill Lane
Elkton, MD 21921